IN DUARTE'S
HOMELAND

by Reyes-Mariano, Miguel A.

Edited-Illustrated by O. Wang

– A Stage Play in Three Acts –

Originally written at age 12 by this author

Once seen through a 12-year-old's eyes, this story
was revisited by this same writer as an adult

1

Edited and illustrated by O. Wang
Proofread by Laura Antram – lauraantram@gmail.com
First edition: April. 26th, 1974. Rev. 09.17.2014

LIBRARY OF CONGRESS CATALOGING IN PUBLICATIONS DATA
Reyes-Mariano, Miguel A.

In Duarte's Homeland: a stage-play in three acts. Set on a construction site in Santo Domingo, the capital of the Dominican Republic, the play follows three construction workers—Rafael, Oscar, and Julio—as they face emotional and existential challenges while considering the possibility of migrating to the United States during the 1990s or 2000s. Driven by dreams of a better life in San Juan, Puerto Rico, or New York City, but held back by poverty. They share memories, fears, and hopes while working under the Caribbean sun. Still, their plans to leave are both made and broken too, with a fall, a betrayal, shadows of doubt, and tests of their relationships as each must confront their future and what they are willing to walk away from. The play blurs the line between reality and truth, exploring migration not as a solution, but as a catalyst for change. This is so because dignity surrounds those who are building the world and longing to escape their circumstances to become better human beings.

ISBN on Back-Cover
Printed in the United States of America

Table of Contents

4

Preface

This story is told through the eyes of a 12-year-old boy—wide-eyed, eager, and perhaps a little too curious for his own good. At that age, when the world feels like a strange stage, and every moment holds the possibility of something being discovered, lost, or broken. This isn't just a childhood story, but a journey from that initial sense of wonder to the complex reflections of an adult looking back while navigating the complexities of human resettlement in the 21st century.

The original version of this story—its sketches, images, characters, and mood—came alive during a time when the world still felt freshly painted in bold colors. It was imagined between school recesses and dusty construction sites, amid the swirl of overheard adult conversations and secret friendships. Thanks to the fact that this writer's father was a Civil Engineer. Nonetheless, what you are about to read is a reinterpretation of that original spirit, filtered now through the lens of adulthood, with its accumulated weight of memory, nuance, and the bitter knowledge that some things are not as they seemed.

Growing up in the Dominican Republic, I lived in a space where physical and imagined borders blurred, as almost three million people of Dominican origin live in the United States. So, the actual walls of my school and home, the frontier with Haiti, and the mental barriers that defined who belonged where, and the dreamlike flow of stories passed down from neighbors, whispered behind shutters during blackouts, or smuggled across radio static and bootleg cassette tapes. Every alley, every half-built house, every rooster's cry before dawn was a gateway to something else. And that "something else" lived inside me just as much as it existed in the world around me. Not to mention that one of my uncles, "Tio Enrique," never came back home (probably from trying to get to Puerto Rico through the Mona Canal.

Thus, be aware that the story you hold in your hands was initially written in a voice free from critical theory and literary pretensions. It was an instinctive narrative, alive with the raw urgency of a boy's desire to understand why people leave, why others stay, and why some never manage to do either. But as time passes, we change. The boy becomes a man, the man wanders and returns—physically, emotionally, and linguistically—and discovers that the questions haven't gone away. They've simply become more complex.

This reinterpretation does not seek to silence that child but to honor him.

He was the one who paid attention when adults thought no one was listening. He was the one who made up entire conversations between pigeons and laborers, who gave mythological meanings to coins in the street, and dreamed up whole life stories for the strangers waiting in bus terminals. He didn't yet know about migration statistics, postcolonial theory, or the economics of belonging. But he felt them in his bones.

And now, through the grown-up voice of that same boy—older, yes, but not yet fully wise-those early impulses resurface with greater clarity. We now see what was buried beneath the surface: the class tensions, the colonial echoes, the buried griefs, and the impossible dreams of financial freedom. We revisit that job site not only as a physical place but as a metaphor for identity-in-progress: always half-built, constantly in need of rebar to support the weight of history and memory.

In crafting this reinterpretation, I granted that child full permission to speak again—but also allowed the adult to respond, correct, and add shadows and silence where necessary. What emerged was not a memoir but something closer to a palimpsest. You will notice traces of the original underneath. Sometimes they are bright, naive strokes of humor and wonder; other times, they peek through with unintentional cruelty or confused longing. I try not to edit these out, but let them out as initially idealized. They are part of the truth.

The adult narrator knows things the child does not: the outcome of certain choices, the consequences of silence, and the beauty of nuance. He understands the pain of nostalgia and the risk of idealizing the past. Yet, even he still clings to certain illusions—still wonders, still mourns, and still listens for stories within the hum of everyday life.

This new revised version of the story exists in that liminal space between memory and imagination. It is a conversation across time: the child speaking in dreams, the adult responding in prose.

To help contemporary readers understand, it might be useful to see this work through the lens of "double consciousness," a term from W.E.B. Du Bois—not only related to race or culture but also to time and emotion. There is the awareness of the boy and the awareness of the man. There is the story as it was initially imagined and the story as it is now remembered and rewritten. As literary scholar Marianne Hirsch (1997) describes in her idea of "postmemory," our connection to the past—especially one we didn't fully understand at the time—is shaped not by direct memories, but by the stories we keep telling ourselves about what happened. This book is such a story.

Readers familiar with the Dominican diaspora will recognize the emotional map etched in these pages. Those unfamiliar may gain insight into the layered experiences of people who carry one foot in their homeland and the other on borrowed soil of Washington Heights (Dominicans' diaspora). This emotional geography includes Santo Domingo, San Juan, and a tiny portion of New York City—not as fixed settings, but as shifting symbols of hope, abandonment, reinvention, and betrayal. These are not cities in the tourist brochure sense. They are psychological zones of transit and transformation.

Yet, this story isn't just about physical migration. It's about the emotional transitions we all experience—between childhood and adulthood, between certainty and doubt, and between what we were told and what we discover on our own. If you've ever stood in a place you once knew well and realized it no longer recognizes you, then this book may be speaking to you as well.

Stylistically, you'll notice moments of magical realism—an inheritance from my cultural storytelling traditions, where supernatural elements were never opposed to realism but existed within it. As García

Márquez once said, "What matters in life is not what happens to you but what you remember and how you remember it." This work makes no claim to factual consistency. Memory rarely does. Even when its plot might follow a linear path, it's not so for the emotional journey of the characters.

In some passages, a character may appear who has already vanished. A ghost might speak more truthfully than a living person. A city could become a character itself, pulling dreams into its core. That is intentional. This story was never meant to be tamed. Its form follows the logic of memory, not the logic of a travel itinerary or a government migration policy. Time folds and unfolds as needed. The heart moves to its own rhythm.

To readers coming of age now, in a time when global movement is both more common and more politically charged than ever before, I offer this book as both a mirror and a map. It does not claim to have answers. Instead, it offers a series of questions—some raw, others wrapped in metaphor, all of them alive...

Why do people leave the only homes they've ever known?

What do we carry with us that we should have left behind?

What does it mean to belong somewhere, and who gets to decide?

These aren't abstract philosophical dilemmas. They are daily questions for many people. For a child, they might appear as whispered worries at night. For an adult, they can crop up in the middle of a quiet afternoon, disguised as a sigh, a scent, or a sudden urge to rewrite a story told differently before.

I hope that you, the reader—wherever you are in your own story—will find something here that resonates or perhaps helps you better understand the otherness theory. Not because our lives are the same, but because we all have that child inside us who once wondered, imagined, or misunderstood the grown-up world and kept trying to make sense of it.

This book is the child's second chance to explore the intricacies of this material world.

And it is mine too.

Miguel A. Reyes-Mariano
September 17th, 2014
Buffalo, New York

List of Characters

Main Characters

These three characters carry the emotional weight and dramatic arc of the entire play:

RAFAEL

- o Age: 40s
- o Role: The oldest and most grounded of the trio; serves as the philosophical and emotional anchor.
- o Traits: Stoic, poetic, world-weary, deeply introspective.
- o Arc: Though he dreams of leaving, he ultimately chooses to stay, becoming a keeper of memory and identity.
- o Symbolism: Represents roots, memory, and the quiet strength of those who remain behind.

OSCAR

- o Age: 30s
- o Role: The comic relief with depth; he bridges the emotional extremes of Rafael and Julio.

- Traits: Sarcastic, vibrant, loyal, emotionally conflicted.

- Arc: Torn between staying and going, he ultimately leans toward leaving but is still suspended in indecision.

- Symbolism: Embodies transition, restlessness, and the liminal state between past and future.

JULIO

- Age: Mid-20s

- Role: The youngest and most hopeful; the one who initiates movement and eventual departure.

- Traits: Dreamer, idealistic, impulsive, vulnerable.

- Arc: From dreaming of migration to actually boarding the ferry, Julio is the play's emotional spark and forward motion.

- Symbolism: Represents hope, change, and the future generation's hunger for more.

Secondary Characters (Implied or Referenced)

These figures are never seen on stage but deeply influence the story and the inner lives of the main characters:

Julio's Mother

- o Referenced as someone Julio wants to support by migrating.
- o Symbol of love, responsibility, and the reasons people endure hardship.

Oscar's Mother and Sister

- o His mother represents memory and inherited wisdom ("no somos tierra seca").
- o His sister, indirectly, embodies the familial bonds that migration threatens to stretch or break.

Rafael's Father and Brother

- o Father is referenced multiple times as a source of strength and poetic wisdom.
- o Brother left the island years ago, representing the forked path Rafael never took.

The "Capitan"/Captain

- o A shadowy ferry smuggler figure. Never appears, but looms large in the migration plan.

- o Represents the danger and murky ethics of illegal migration.

Julio's Cousins / Oscar's uncle Leo / Rafael's Cousin in New Jersey

- o Each of these minor characters adds personal migration stories that texture the larger theme of departure and identity transformation.

"The Island" (as a voice/character)

- o In "The Island That Listens", the land itself becomes a sentient, almost mythic character, warning against forgetting one's roots.

- o Represents cultural memory, ancestral legacy, and the soul of home.

The Cement, Sweat, & Burden of Hopes comes together in a heartfelt play—Dr. T. Pires Zalla

Prologue

(Lights up on an empty construction site—The hum of waves and distant traffic in the background. A lone piece of rebar stands center stage, upright in the dirt like a forgotten flagpole. A single voice, RAFAEL or a NARRATOR, steps forward and speaks directly to the audience. His tone is quiet, steady—like someone reciting something sacred and worn.)

NARRATOR / RAFAEL:

We begin where the sun doesn't ask questions.

Where cement is poured over other people's dreams,

And men become ghosts before their shift ends

Here, in Santo Domingo,

A shovel is your dignity,

and a ferry is a rumor told in cash

Here, three men dig

One wants to leave

One swears he's ready

One holds the map, and no one can read aloud

They mix concrete and fantasy

Carry buckets full of doubt

They argue over things no border can explain—

Like what it means to vanish in search of yourself

You'll meet them:
Julio runs before his shadow catches up
Oscar, who buys hope in plastic and prayer
And me—Rafael—who remembers what others
forget

This isn't a story of arrival
Not really
It's the story of standing on the rooftop of your life,
And asking if jumping is the same as flying

What follows is a ladder
It creaks. It leans
And sometimes, it breaks

But if you listen closely,
You'll hear what the island says before we say
goodbye

(Lights dim. The hum of waves and distant traffic fades in. Transition into Act I, Scene 1.)

Act One – Foundations and Farewells

Setting: A dusty construction site in Santo Domingo. Conversations mix with daydreams and buried memories.

I. Shovel and Sunlight

Introduction to the workers and their routine; banter masks deeper longings.

Scene: Mid-morning sun slices through a humid haze. The three men work side by side under a mango tree by a half-built house. Cement buckets clink, shovels scrape, and laughter breaks the monotony. To the East side of the construction site, it is possible to see a full-grown Mangoes tree in the background.

RAFAEL (40s), stoic but dryly humorous, takes a long drag from a bottle of water.

RAFAEL

You know, if we dig just a few more meters, we might hit San Juan straight from here.

OSCAR (30s), wiry and talkative, slaps his shovel into the dirt.

OSCAR

Ha! That would save me a boat ride and a coyote's cut. You sure it doesn't lead to the Chinese?
JULIO (mid-20s), the youngest, wipes sweat from his forehead, hopeful eyes scanning the horizon.

                    JULIO
I'll take either. China or San Juan. Just as long as it's not here.

                    RAFAEL
You're still green, Julio. You think anywhere's better than home.

                    OSCAR
Tell me, Rafa, if home is so good, why does your passport sleep under your pillow?

                    RAFAEL (grinning)
To remind me I still have choices. Not everyone's stuck like rebar in concrete.

                    JULIO
Choices? You've been saying you're leaving for two years now. What's holding you? Your dog?

                    RAFAEL
Nah, she left me. Took the dog too.

                    OSCAR

Even the dog got a visa before you! Oh my God!

RAFAEL
Laugh it up. At least I didn't spend all my savings trying to bribe that ferry guy in Samana.

OSCAR (offended)
It was a "processing fee," thank you very much. He had connections!

JULIO
Connections to your wallet, maybe.

OSCAR
Look, laugh all you want, but one day I'll be sipping café in the Floridita in Washington Heights or the Bronx, watching the snow fall like powdered sugar.

RAFAEL
Yeah, while working in a bodega next to a heater and dreaming of avocado trees.

JULIO (serious)
I don't want to dream anymore. I want to go. Puerto Rico first. Then New York City or Perth Amboy in New Jersey.

RAFAEL (pausing work)

You think the world's waiting for you with open
arms?

JULIO

No. But it's not slapping me with this heat and paying
me 500 pesos, just 10 US dollars a day, either.

OSCAR

He's got a point. Yesterday, my nephew sent me a
picture. He's working construction in Queens. He's
got a hard hat, gloves, and — get this — lunch breaks.

RAFAEL

Lunch breaks? Such luxury! What's next, dental
insurance?

OSCAR

Laugh, old man. But he's sending dollars home.
Dollars. My sister built an entire second floor with
what he sent in a year.

JULIO

And here we are — building other people's dreams,
concrete block by block.

RAFAEL (softly)

Don't forget; dreams are heavy too!

OSCAR

So's this damn bucket. Keep dreaming and pass me
that mix.

JULIO (looking up)
Do you think we're just lazy for staying?
RAFAEL
Lazy? No. Tired maybe. Or scared.

OSCAR
Speak for yourself. I've packed twice. Left notes. Said goodbye. Still here.

RAFAEL
Maybe you like the drama.

OSCAR
Maybe I like not drowning.

JULIO
So, we all want out, but we're all still here?

RAFAEL
That's the curse. You love the land, but it doesn't love you back the way it should.

OSCAR
Like my ex.

RAFAEL
Did she get a green card too?

OSCAR
No, she got a "gringo" (an American). Same result.

JULIO (smirking)
Maybe I should find myself a "gringa" (American girl)
RAFAEL
You? You barely survive your cousin's cooking. You'd die on foreign food alone.

JULIO
I'd die full of dreams. That's better than starving here.

OSCAR (after a pause)
Hey, do you guys ever imagine it? Like... close your eyes and see yourself already there?

RAFAEL
Sometimes. I see myself in a coat. Snow on my beard. Carrying a toolbox to a job that pays in dollars. Not pesos.

OSCAR
I see myself in the subway, headphones on, walking fast like I've got a purpose. You know?

JULIO
I see my mom's smile when I send her money. Fix the roof. Buy her meds. That's what I see.

RAFAEL (quietly)
That's the real migration—our thoughts get there before we do.

OSCAR

26

Meanwhile, our bodies keep mixing cement.

RAFAEL
Shovel and sunlight. That's today. What's tomorrow?

JULIO
Boat ticket. Puerto Rico. That's my plan.

OSCAR
Are you serious?

JULIO (nods)
Talked to a guy in the sector of "El Conde." He knows someone. I'm meeting him Saturday.

RAFAEL
Careful. Most of those guys know how to take your hope and sell it back to you twice the price.

JULIO
It's a risk. But it's mine to take.

OSCAR
If you make it... send us pictures of snow, eh?

JULIO
No. I'll send you a ticket.

RAFAEL (smiling faintly)
Just don't forget the ones still mixing cement under the sun.

II. The Map Beneath the Cement

A casual mention of leaving triggers intense personal visions.

Scene: Late afternoon sun bleeds over rebar and half-poured concrete. The three men—RAFAEL, OSCAR, and JULIO—wipe sweat and sling banter while mixing cement. Dust rises in clouds. A low radio plays a "salsarengue" song somewhere in the distance.

OSCAR
(Slapping the wheelbarrow)
If I make it out of here, first stop: Puerto Rico. Second stop: The Bronx. Third stop: therapy.

RAFAEL
(Laughing)
Therapy? What for?

OSCAR
For this back! And maybe for the trauma of fifteen years under this damn sun.

JULIO
You? Bronx? Nah, you're more of a Washington

Heights kind of guy—loud, stubborn, and impossible
to ignore.

OSCAR

I'll take that as a compliment. The Bronx got flavor.
And better bodegas.

RAFAEL

And gunshots, too.

OSCAR

Please. That's just fireworks from failed dreams.

JULIO

(Suddenly quiet)
You ever think... what if you never leave?

RAFAEL

(Stops mixing, looks over)
Every day.

OSCAR

That's dark, Julio.

JULIO

It's real.

RAFAEL

You know what's real? This cement. This heat. That
foreman who always smells like onions.

OSCAR

(Laughs)

Facts.

JULIO

I mean it. What if we keep dreaming and never move?
What if this *is* it?

OSCAR

Then I want a refund for my imagination.

RAFAEL

(Softly)

Your imagination's the only passport most of us will
ever hold.

JULIO

(Sits on a pile of blocks)

I see it sometimes. I close my eyes and boom—I'm
standing on a subway platform. Not here. There. You
know?

OSCAR

Yeah. Cold air, smells like wet metal and coffee. A girl
walks by with a scarf and headphones, doesn't even
look at me. And somehow... I belong.

RAFAEL

I see the same platform. But empty. No people. Just
me and echoes. Like I made it, but no one's waiting.

OSCAR

Damn, old man. That's heavy.

RAFAEL

Dreams can weigh more than cement.

JULIO

I had this dream last week. I was in a snowstorm. My boots were soaked. I was holding a photo of my mom, but it kept getting wet, the ink running down. I couldn't read her face.

OSCAR

(Pauses)

Have you ever dream you're back here, but different? Like, you made it—but you come back with clean shoes, and people look at you like a ghost?

RAFAEL

Yeah. Like you made it out, but left something behind you can't name.

JULIO

Or someone.

(Silence falls. The cement mixer churns like a mechanical heartbeat.)

OSCAR

You know what's under this cement?

RAFAEL

Rats?

OSCAR

(Laughs)

No, I mean under *all* of this. The ground. The layers.
It's like a map.

JULIO

A map?

OSCAR

Yeah. Of who we were. Childhoods. Secrets. Places we
wanted to escape.

RAFAEL

So we're paving over memory?

OSCAR

Maybe. Maybe we're sealing it in like time capsules.
Who knows?

JULIO

When I was seven, I used to think that if I dug deep
enough, I'd hit gold.

RAFAEL

You hit rocks and maybe some worms.

JULIO

Nah. I hit an old doll once. Half melted. No eyes. Still haunts me.

OSCAR

You're haunted by plastic. I'm haunted by choices.

RAFAEL

We all are. My cousin left some years ago. Jumped on a boat to Mayagüez. Said he'd be back in a year. He never came back.

JULIO

Where'd he go?

RAFAEL

New Jersey. Has a pizza place now. Sends postcards with snow and smiling kids.

OSCAR

Sounds like a success story.

RAFAEL

Sure. But his mom died waiting. Every birthday, she cooked his favorite stew in case he might show up.

JULIO

Oof. That's tough, you!

OSCAR

That's the price. You make it there, but parts of you

stay behind. Like roots that still grow, even if the tree's been cut.

JULIO

Still worth it?

RAFAEL

Ask me when I've gone.

OSCAR

I used to trace maps in school. With a pencil. Follow the lines with my finger. I'd whisper names like "Brooklyn" and "Orlando" like prayers.

JULIO

Me too. I circled New York City so many times that my textbook had a hole in it.

RAFAEL

And yet here we are. Still tracing maps, just with sweat and broken nails.

OSCAR

You think maybe the real map's in our heads?

JULIO

Or our feet. Always itching to move.

RAFAEL

You know what I envy?

OSCAR

Besides my good looks?

RAFAEL

Julio's hope. It's loud. It hasn't been beaten quiet yet.

JULIO

Don't envy me. I'm terrified. Every day. I'm scared I'll leave and fail. Scared I'll stay and rot.

OSCAR

That's honest.

RAFAEL

That's courage.

(A gust of wind blows dust over the site. The men squint, then return to work. But their minds linger elsewhere.)

OSCAR

If I ever leave, I'll tattoo the island on my back. Just so I never forget where I came from.

RAFAEL

Better put it on your chest. So, when you hug someone, they feel it.

JULIO

I'll put it on my feet. So, it walks with me wherever I go.

OSCAR

That's beautiful, bro.

RAFAEL

That's the kind of poetry only pain can write.

(The cement sets. The mixer groans to a stop. Above the drying slab, laughter fades into thoughts — heavy, fragile, and shaped like elsewhere.)

III. Ghosts of Duarte

National pride, family struggles, and generational hopes emerge.

Scene: A little later, same afternoon. The shadows stretch long across the site. Dust swirls with each shuffle of boots. The radio hums a "merengue" song, half-drowned by the clang of shovels and rebar.

RAFAEL

(Leaning on his shovel, squinting toward the horizon)
You ever think what Duarte would say if he saw this mess?

OSCAR

(Smacking a cement bag)

He'd probably ask for a refund. Or a machete.

JULIO

(Laughing)

Or a visa.

RAFAEL

Nah. Duarte wouldn't leave. He'd stand on a crate
and shout, "Wake up, Dominicans, damn!"

OSCAR

And the people would keep scrolling on their phones.

RAFAEL

(Lowers his head)

We forget too easily. That man died broke in
Venezuela, dreaming of this country. And now look at
us—dreaming of other countries to survive.

JULIO

Well, pride doesn't pay rent. You think my mother
cares about flags when the fridge is empty?

RAFAEL

That's not the point. Pride is what keeps your back
straight when the world wants you to bend.

OSCAR

Straight backs still break under weight, my bro.

JULIO

But what weight did Duarte carry? No kids, no house,
no cement mixing under the sun.

RAFAEL

He carried vision. And vision doesn't get old. It just
waits in silence until someone sees it again.

OSCAR

Like a ghost.

JULIO

A ghost with a beard and a permanent spot on our
pesos.

RAFAEL

More than that. He's in how my grandma used to
hang the flag every February 27th, like it was sacred
cloth. How she made me stand still for the anthem,
even when the power was out.

OSCAR

(Laughs softly)

I remember that. My father used to yell at the TV
during Independence Day parades. "They forgot the
real heroes," he'd say. "These men in suits are just
actors."

RAFAEL

He wasn't wrong.

JULIO

You think we're just actors, too?

RAFAEL

No. We're the backstage crew. Lifting the country behind the scenes.

OSCAR

For no applause.

JULIO

Just calloused hands and back pain.

OSCAR

And second jobs.

RAFAEL

But maybe that's the point. Maybe Duarte wasn't dreaming of a country with suits and slogans. Perhaps he dreamed of us. The builders. The believers.

JULIO

(Sits on a bag of sand)

My grandfather fought in the April Revolution of 1965. Said he saw Americans land in tanks and planes. He told me once, "I gave my youth to a flag that still forgets my name."

RAFAEL

That's the wound, isn't it? We carry their struggle, but not their place.

OSCAR

My uncle left for Puerto Rico in the late '80s. Sent cassette tapes to us. I remember his voice crackling through the stereo. Always ended with "Take care of the homeland." I didn't even know what that meant at the time.

RAFAEL

It means you still love the land, even when it spits in your face.

JULIO

My little brother doesn't even know who Duarte is. Thinks it's the name of a street.

OSCAR

Well... he's not wrong.

RAFAEL

But it's more than asphalt. It's the Dominican's story. Memory. Sacrifices.

OSCAR

And ghosts.

JULIO

Maybe that's what Santo Domingo is now—ghosts buried under concrete and dreams.

RAFAEL

Sometimes I think my father's voice is buried under this dust. He used to say, "Don't let this place harden your heart. Build something softer inside."

OSCAR

Did he?

RAFAEL

Tried. Died with a busted spine and unpaid bills, but he died believing this country could still be something.

JULIO

I envy that kind of belief.

OSCAR

Me too. Mine's thinner now. More... negotiable.

RAFAEL

But you still show up. That's belief in motion.

JULIO

You know what I hope? That my kids don't have to mix cement in another man's country. That they can dream in Spanish and still get paid with dignity.

OSCAR

Amen to that.

RAFAEL

I hope they remember us, not as the ones who ran,
but the ones who endured.

JULIO

You think history will remember us?

OSCAR

History doesn't remember men with shovels unless
they throw them.

RAFAEL

Then we throw them upward—into something better.

JULIO

Into the sky?

RAFAEL

Into the next chapter. Even if we don't get to read it.

OSCAR

That's the thing about ghosts. They linger in stories
we tell, not statues we forget.

**(The men are silent. A car horn blares nearby. The
sun lowers, brushing the horizon in orange. A
breeze carries dust and a strange, almost nostalgic
scent.)**

RAFAEL

You feel that?

JULIO

What?

RAFAEL

That moment. Like something old just passed through
us.

OSCAR

Maybe Duarte himself. Checking in.

JULIO

If he is, he had better bring water.

RAFAEL

No. He'd bring firewood. To remind us to keep the
flame lit.

OSCAR

Even when it burns?

RAFAEL

Especially then.

(The workers pick up their tools again. The site
returns to motion, but their minds remain wrapped
in flags, stories, and fading voices that still whisper
through Santo Domingo's cracked walls.)

IV. The Rooftop Pact

They secretly agree to leave for Puerto Rico
together. gringo

**Scene: The golden hour. The men sit on the
unfinished rooftop, legs dangling over the edge. The
city murmurs below—"motoconchos" moving
around, kids shout in alleyways, and a church bell
rings somewhere in the distance. They pass a plastic
bottle of warm soda back and forth between them.
The cement beneath them still holds the day's heat.**

JULIO
(Quietly)
Feels different up here. Like the noise down there
isn't mine to carry anymore.

OSCAR
Uhmm! From up here, the city looks... calm. Like it's
pretending to be something it's not.

RAFAEL
Everything's pretending. Us too.

JULIO
You think so?

44

RAFAEL

Sure. We pretend we're just working. That we're fine. That tomorrow's going to feel any different than today...

OSCAR

(Sips)

Damn, Rafa. That soda went dark.

RAFAEL

Truth's bitter, brother.

JULIO

But we're not just pretending. I mean—I've been saving. Little by little.

OSCAR

For Puerto Rico?

JULIO

Yeah. I got a guy. Says he can get me on a cargo boat in Boca Chica. Leaves in two weeks. Small crew. Quiet operation.

RAFAEL

Two weeks?

OSCAR

You trust him?

JULIO

No. But I trust I can't stay here.

RAFAEL

(Leans back, staring at the fading sun)
You know, back in '79, I almost left, too. Had everything ready. My brother backed out the night before. Said Mami cried too hard. I stayed. He left.

OSCAR

Where's he now?

RAFAEL

Brooklyn. Two kids. Divorced. Says sometimes he misses the Dominican "quipes" more than his ex-wife.

JULIO

So, why would you want to go after that?

RAFAEL

I got used to staying. Staying becomes a kind of rust.

OSCAR

You ever regret it?

RAFAEL

Every time I smell ocean and wind, I know it ain't taking me nowhere.

(A long pause. Wind rustles loose tarps. Julio's leg swings slightly over the edge.)

OSCAR

I've been thinking about it too. For real this time. Not just talking over lunch.

JULIO

You serious?

OSCAR

Yeah. I got a cousin in Mayagüez. Works landscaping. Says he can line up something for me, under the table.

RAFAEL

So you both have routes. And I'm just the guy with a shovel and an expired dream.

OSCAR

Don't do that. You're still strong. You could make it.

RAFAEL

Strength won't get me past the Coast Guard.

JULIO

But maybe unity will.

RAFAEL

Unity?

JULIO

What if we go together?

OSCAR

(Whistles softly)

Now that's something.

JULIO

Three of us. We plan it right. Share the costs. Watch each other's backs. Three sets of eyes, three sets of hands.

RAFAEL

You sound like you already made the pact.

JULIO

I have. In my head. Every night before bed.

OSCAR

(Claps his hands softly)

Then let's say it out loud.

RAFAEL

Say what?

OSCAR

That we'll go. Together. Leave this rooftop for real, not just in conversation.

JULIO

Rafa?

RAFAEL

(Looks at his hands, rough and cracked)

I've built a hundred homes for other people. Maybe it's time I build a new life for myself.

OSCAR

That's a yes?

RAFAEL

That's a *hell* yes.

(The three men exchange a look—equal parts thrill and fear.)

JULIO

We keep it between us. No family, no girlfriends, no drinking buddies.

OSCAR

Loose mouths sink boats.

RAFAEL

Literally.

JULIO

We pool our money. I'll talk to my guy again. If it sounds solid, we lock it in.

OSCAR

We meet every other night. Right here. Rooftop council.

RAFAEL

Agreed.

JULIO

And no backing out. We hold each other to this.

OSCAR

Blood oath?

RAFAEL

Relax. A word is enough.

JULIO

For now. But if someone starts doubting, we speak up. No disappearing, no cold feet.

OSCAR

What about papers? IDs?

JULIO

They won't ask. Cargo crew wants silence, not scrutiny. We'll be "mechanics," apparently.

RAFAEL

I can fix a hammer. Close enough.

(They laugh, but it's tight—nervous.)

OSCAR

You think it'll be better?

RAFAEL

Different. That's enough.

JULIO

I don't need riches. Just a roof, I don't pour for
someone else.

OSCAR

Or the streets I walk on without feeling stuck.

RAFAEL

I just want to stop waking up tired before I even start.

**(They sit in silence again. Below them, the city
sputters and hums — alive but unchanging.)**

JULIO

To the pact, then.

OSCAR

To the leap.

RAFAEL

To leaving shadows behind.

**(They each spit into their palms and shake — a quiet,
primal bond.)**

RAFAEL

This rooftop just became sacred ground.

OSCAR

We'll look back on it one day and say: *That* was where
we were reborn.

JULIO

Or at least where we stopped pretending.

(They remain there until the last light dies. Three silhouettes against a shifting sky, no longer waiting—now preparing.)

Act Two – Sea of Promises

Setting: Mental landscapes, imagined border crossings, ferry rides, and migration stories—real or fictional—intertwine.

V. Crossing Without Moving

One imagines boarding the ferry to Mayagüez; others join in, suspending disbelief.

Scene: Midday on another day. Cement buckets rest, shovels stuck in place. The men take a break under a partially built overhang, the ocean breeze faint in the distance. Sweat evaporates slowly on their skin. But in their minds—they are somewhere else.

JULIO
You know what I did last night?

RAFAEL
Judging by your face—nothing legal.

JULIO
(Laughs)

No, seriously. I closed my eyes and boarded the ferry.

Like for real. I imagined the floor vibrating beneath my feet, the salty air in my nose. The whole thing.

OSCAR

You dreamed the Mayagüez ferry?

JULIO

Not a dream. More like... rehearsal.

RAFAEL

Go on then. Walk us through it. Let's sail without crossing the Mona passage.

JULIO

Alright. Picture this: 2:15 a.m., Boca de Yuma. The moon's a slice. You're shivering, not from cold, but from nerves. You hear your name whispered—not yelled—because everything's quiet, like the sea's holding its breath.

OSCAR

Who's calling?

JULIO

Some skinny guy with too much gel. Calls himself the "Capitan." Has one flip-flop and a limp.

RAFAEL

(Laughing)
That tracks.

JULIO

He nods, points to the boat. Not a ferry like in the brochure. Nah. It's more like a boat painted blue twelve years ago.

OSCAR

I can smell the diesel already.

JULIO

Exactly! The whole thing stinks—oil, fear, and fish. You step on, and it rocks like it doesn't want you there.

RAFAEL

Sounds like my ex's bed.

OSCAR

God help us.

JULIO

So we sit. Three of us. Shoulder to shoulder. No talking. Just the hum of the engine. You start to count waves, but they're all the same. That's when it hits you—we're not going back.

RAFAEL

Damn. That's a feeling.

OSCAR

I see it too now. My legs are cramping. There's a guy

behind me whispering a prayer in Haitian Creole. I don't understand the words, but I feel them.

JULIO

Yes! And then someone pukes over the side.

RAFAEL

Of course. That's tradition. Thankfully, the waves are calm, and the trip goes without any incidents.

OSCAR

And then it's sunrise. Faint gold rising behind clouds. Maybe 18 hours later... Did you spot land?

JULIO

Mayagüez. Faded cranes. Palm trees. A tired dock.

RAFAEL

And no one claps. No celebration. Just quiet relief.

JULIO

Exactly. But when you step off, it feels like your legs forgot how to walk on land. The air smells different. Sweeter. Less dust, more... plastic and pastry.

OSCAR

You look around, and suddenly you're not "Julio from Herrera." You're "someone else's cousin," a shadow with a backpack.

RAFAEL

A number. A maybe.

OSCAR

I go to the payphone. Call my cousin. But the coins don't work. Voice on the other end says, ¿Who is this?

JULIO

"It's me."

RAFAEL

But "me" doesn't mean much there. "Me" needs proof. "Me" needs a ride. "Me" needs work.

JULIO

Still... I'd do it. Even in my shoes now, even barefoot.

OSCAR

Have I ever told you about my uncle Leo? He didn't take a ferry. Swam part of it. Half-crazy. Says he tied his passport in a sandwich bag to his ankle.

RAFAEL

Is he still in Puerto Rico?

OSCAR

No. He made it all the way to Lynn, Massachusetts. Got a snowplow job. Says the snow is cleaner than politics.

JULIO

That's poetic.

RAFAEL

Alright. My turn.

JULIO

Let's hear it.

RAFAEL

We're not on a boat. We're walking. We somehow made it. We crossed the Guatemala-Mexico border. Passing through it mainly at night. Through hills. A king of walking with no maps, only whispers. Even the leaves crunch differently. There's fog.

OSCAR

Fog?

RAFAEL

Yeah. And silence. Not peaceful silence—the kind that makes you look back every ten steps.

JULIO

Do we have guides?

RAFAEL

A boy. Couldn't be older than fifteen. Says nothing the whole time. Just points. And when we finally reach the clearing—bam. There's a clearing with a wire fence. That's the line. The border. But there's no sign, no welcome.

OSCAR

Do we cross?

RAFAEL

We hesitate. Then we look at each other. We link arms. And we step over.

JULIO

Just like that?

RAFAEL

Just like that. And the air? It doesn't feel different. But inside—it's like we just breathed for the first time.

OSCAR

You ever think maybe we've already crossed?

JULIO

What do you mean?

OSCAR

I mean... in our heads. Every day we imagine it. Live it. Taste it. Perhaps we've been mentally migrating for years.

RAFAEL

Crossing without moving.

JULIO

That should be a song.

RAFAEL

Or a confession.

OSCAR

Either way, it's real.

(They sit in silence. The half-built wall behind them casts a jagged shadow.)

RAFAEL

Sometimes I wonder if the real border is fear.

JULIO

And if we cross it... what's on the other side?

OSCAR

Us. But freer. Or at least—different.

JULIO

Next week, I'm meeting the ferry guy again. For real.

OSCAR

You want us with you?

RAFAEL

Or behind you?

JULIO

With me. Always.

(They nod. No more pretending. The ferry may be imaginary today—but the crossing begins with belief.)

VI. San Juan Mirage

Fantasies of arrival, jobs, and betrayals in Puerto Rico blur into memory.

Scene: Late afternoon at the job site. Dust hangs in the golden light. The three men take shelter on stacked wooden planks beneath a half-finished wall. Work pauses—but their minds keep going.

JULIO
Alright. Picture it. We arrive in San Juan. Ferry door creaks open, and we step out like saints. Tired, hungry saints.

OSCAR
(Laughing)
Speak for yourself. I'm stepping off like a millionaire with amnesia.

RAFAEL
You're both delusional. That dock smells like fish and sweat. You'll arrive as a ghost. No one claps at your landing.

JULIO

But I'll be standing. On new soil. Isn't that enough?

OSCAR

Not when your cousin forgets to pick you up.

RAFAEL

Again?

OSCAR

Happened to my brother. Slept two nights in a baseball dugout near Bayamon. Said the mosquitoes there have teeth.

JULIO

Then we don't wait for cousins. We find our own path. We hit the Street Loiza, ask for work, keep moving.

RAFAEL

What kind of work?

JULIO

Anything. Kitchens, loading docks, cleaning rooms in motels with names like "Sol y Luna."

OSCAR

I got a motel story.

RAFAEL

Of course you do.

OSCAR

My uncle got a job mopping floors at this run-down place near Carolina. The owner promised cash every Friday. The first week, he got twenty-five dollars and a bucket of expired crackers.

JULIO

That's robbery.

OSCAR

He stayed six months.

RAFAEL

Why?

OSCAR

Said it was still better than the silence in his house back here.

JULIO

Sometimes even crumbs taste sweet if you've been starving long enough.

RAFAEL

You think San Juan is some shining city?

JULIO

No. I think it's complicated. But it's a place I haven't failed yet.

OSCAR

Uhmm! I picture myself arriving, finding a job at some bakery. Owner's half-blind, so he doesn't check papers.

RAFAEL

You'd eat all the bread.

OSCAR

Only the guava pastries. And maybe a co-worker named Marisol.

JULIO

(Laughing)
You're hopeless.

RAFAEL

I had a cousin—Maribel—who made it to San Juan. Started working in a beauty salon. Got her papers through a fake marriage.

OSCAR

She's lucky, ah?

RAFAEL

She thought so. Until the guy who married her started showing up drunk. Called her "my maid" in front of people.

JULIO

That's cold.

RAFAEL

Yeah. She left him. Still stayed, though. Said humiliation was just another kind of border she crossed.

OSCAR

That's deep.

RAFAEL

She never came back, even when her mother died.

JULIO

Maybe she couldn't. Or maybe she was afraid that if she returned, she'd never leave again.

OSCAR

So we fantasize about arrivals, but forget what it means to stay.

JULIO

We also forget who we become once we cross. You think we stay the same?

RAFAEL

No. Migration is molting. You shed skin you didn't even know you wore.

OSCAR

You shed names, too. I knew a guy named Sanson who started calling himself "Sam."

JULIO

"Sam"? Like Yosemite Sam?

OSCAR

No—like he wanted to forget where he came from.
Told everyone he was born in Orlando.

RAFAEL

People rewrite their histories like passports.

JULIO

But what if you get stuck between stories? Not here,
not there.

OSCAR

Then you float. You drift.

RAFAEL

Like a ferry with no anchor.

JULIO

In my fantasy, we arrive together. We get jobs at a
furniture warehouse, lifting sofas and beds, laughing
like idiots while hiding from the boss.

OSCAR

We live in a tiny apartment. Roaches have seniority.

RAFAEL

And we share one fan.

JULIO

But we eat rice at night. We call home. We send
money.

OSCAR

And we don't forget who we are.

RAFAEL

That's the hard part. The forgetting happens slowly.
Like erosion.

OSCAR

You wake up one day and don't recognize your own
voice.

JULIO

I'll write letters. To myself. To remember.

RAFAEL

Letters? Who reads letters anymore?

JULIO

I will. On my worst days. I'll open one and read:
"Dear Julio, don't let the cold erase your fire."

OSCAR

I'd write: "Oscar, stay loud. Even if no one
understands you."

RAFAEL

Mine would say: "Rafael, you're more than your hands."

(They fall into silence. The breeze kicks up. Dust swirls at their feet.)

JULIO

You think Puerto Rico's waiting for us?

OSCAR

I think it's ignoring us. Like everywhere else.

RAFAEL

Which means we sneak in like shadows and carve space with sweat.

OSCAR

And we don't trust anyone who smiles too fast.

RAFAEL

Especially if they offer help for a price.

JULIO

But we help each other.

RAFAEL

That's the pact.

OSCAR

Pact still stands.

(They spit into their palms again and stack hands.)

JULIO

To cross the ocean. Even the one inside us.

RAFAEL

To see through mirages.

OSCAR

And building something real—even if it starts in
fantasy.

(The light fades. The city blurs in heat shimmer. But
for a moment, the three men live in a place far from
dust and cement—standing at the edge of San Juan,
whole and unbroken.)

VII. La Sombra del Norte

They argue over what awaits in New York:
salvation, servitude, or erasure.

Scene: Twilight settles over the job site. They sit on
stacked buckets and cinder blocks, the last of the
light brushing the unfinished walls around them.
Nothing moves—except their thoughts.

OSCAR

You know what I saw once? A picture of Times Square at night. All those lights... Man, I thought it looked like heaven cracked open.

JULIO

Or a giant billboard with no soul.

RAFAEL

Depends on who's standing beneath it. Light only blinds if you stare too long.

OSCAR

Don't do that, Rafa. Don't kill the dream before it walks.

RAFAEL

I'm not killing it. I'm just unwrapping it. Dreams rot fast when they stay sealed too long.

JULIO

So what, we don't go?

RAFAEL

I didn't say that. I'm just saying New York isn't salvation. It's not some altar waiting for your sacrifice.

OSCAR

It was for my cousin. He got papers, two jobs, drives a black Accord now.

JULIO

Black Accord doesn't mean peace. I knew a guy in Brooklyn who lived in his car. Said the only thing warm in winter was the lies he told his mother.

OSCAR

You both act like we're marching into a trap.

RAFAEL

A gilded one, maybe. You think you'll arrive and the city will kneel?

OSCAR

No. But it'll give me a shot.

JULIO

And what does that shot cost?

RAFAEL

That's the question nobody asks.

OSCAR

What, you afraid to change?

RAFAEL

I'm afraid of becoming invisible in a place full of light.

JULIO

You think we'll vanish?

RAFAEL

Piece by piece. The name they can't pronounce, the accent they mock, the papers they check twice.

OSCAR

Come on, man. Everyone starts at the bottom.

RAFAEL

Some of us get buried there.

JULIO

(Pauses)

I don't care about the bottom. I just want to know there's more than this.

OSCAR

That's what I'm saying. In New York, you can hustle. You can disappear from who you were and build something new.

RAFAEL

Disappear from who you were? You call that freedom?

OSCAR

Maybe. Or maybe it's mercy. Maybe I don't want to carry this version of myself into the next life.

JULIO

But if you erase everything, what's left?

RAFAEL

Exactly. You spend years becoming someone else, and one day you forget who was the one dreaming in the first place.

OSCAR

That's romantic talk. The world doesn't wait for our identity crisis. It pays you for what you do, not who you are.

RAFAEL

And if you're cleaning toilets with a college degree?

OSCAR

You clean like a king and send money like a saint.

JULIO

(Looking down)

My uncle was a lawyer here. Went to the Bronx. Ended up pushing carts at a supermarket. Never smiled in pictures after that.

OSCAR

So what—he should've stayed?

RAFAEL

No. But maybe he should've known that the North can be colder than snow.

OSCAR

You all keep calling it *the North* like it's a monster in a fable. It's just a place, man.

JULIO

A place that changes people.

RAFAEL

A place that can swallow them.

OSCAR

It also feeds them.

RAFAEL

Only if you're lucky. Or ruthless.

JULIO

Maybe we're all both. I going to share with you guys an article from Onairam Seyer about Dominican immigrants who got ahead thanks to their personal effort (find the article at the end of this play).

(A long pause. A distant horn echoes through the streets below. A dog barks. A plane passes overhead, its blinking lights fading westward.)

JULIO

You know what I dream sometimes?

RAFAEL
What?

JULIO

That I get there. New York. I'm walking past
brownstones in the cold. There's music playing from
a bodega. I stop. And suddenly I miss this — this dust,
this silence, this... nothing.

OSCAR

And then what?

JULIO

And then I cry. But I keep walking.

RAFAEL

That's real.

OSCAR

I dream the opposite. I get there, and I never look
back. I call Ma and say, "I am OK!" Even if I'm not.

JULIO

Why lie?

OSCAR

So she can sleep.

RAFAEL

That's what most migrants carry: dreams and lies.
One for themselves, one for their mothers.

JULIO

Maybe New York is just another name for hunger.

RAFAEL

Or silence. Or reinvention. Or exile.

OSCAR

Or maybe... maybe it's just a mirror. Shows you who you are without the noise.

JULIO

And if you don't like what you see?

RAFAEL

You learn to live with the shadows.

OSCAR

Better than dying under the sun here, dry and invisible.

JULIO

Are we still going?

RAFAEL

Hell yes!

OSCAR

Even after all this?

RAFAEL

Especially after all this. If I'm gonna vanish, at least let it be in motion.

JULIO

Then we walk forward. Into the shadow. Not because
it's easy. But because standing still hurts worse.

RAFAEL

To the North, then. Shadow or not.

OSCAR

We'll light our own way.

(They don't say more. The cement site grows quiet.
But somewhere in the dark, a vision of New York
flickers—not in lights, but in resolve.)

VIII. The Island That Listens

One shares a dream where the land speaks,
warning them of forgetting who they are.

Scene: The construction site is quiet now—just the
crackle of rebar cooling and the rustle of palm
shadows stretching long. The men sit in a triangle
beneath the half-done roof, the air still thick with
imagined salt and the faint echo of ferry horns.

RAFAEL

You ever dream something that feels more real than
your own life?

OSCAR

Every time I dream, I have a mattress with no springs.

JULIO

Or a toilet that can't flush (because there is no water
or the handle is broken, and to repair it is more
expensive than buying a new tank that comes with it).

RAFAEL

I'm serious.

OSCAR

So are we.

RAFAEL

Nah. I mean real... real! Like... it grabs your chest and
doesn't let go when you wake up.

JULIO

Alright, old man. You're making a face. Spill it.

RAFAEL

Last night, I dreamt the island spoke to me.

OSCAR

Spoke? Like... words?

RAFAEL

Yeah. But not with a mouth. It came through everything—the wind, the dirt, even the roosters.

JULIO

(Laughing)

The roosters told you something?

RAFAEL

Mock all you want, but they were as serious as saints.

OSCAR

Okay. I'm listening.

RAFAEL

I was walking through sugarcane fields. But they were taller than me. Towering. And they whispered as I passed, all in this slow, deep tone.

JULIO

What were they saying?

RAFAEL

"Don't forget."

OSCAR

Forget what?

RAFAEL

Don't forget who you are (and it was not the talking monkey of the Lion King). It was more about don't forget where you're rooted. What your roots means when no one's watching.

JULIO

That's some heavy sugarcane, bro.

RAFAEL

Then I found myself at the "Malecon," right? But the sea wasn't moving. Still as glass. And the sky was red. Not sunset red—like warning red.

OSCAR

Like real blood?

RAFAEL

Like memory... and I stepped toward the water, and the land behind me rumbled. I turned, and there were my mother, my abuelo, my childhood home—but crumbling, dissolving like ashes.

JULIO

Damn!...

RAFAEL

And the island said again, but louder this time: "If you leave without listening, you'll forget your name. You'll wear others like masks until none fit."

OSCAR

Man... that sounds like a curse.

RAFAEL

Or a warning.

JULIO

You believe it?

RAFAEL

I don't know. I woke up crying.

OSCAR

I dreamed once that I made it to the Bronx and couldn't speak. Every time I opened my mouth, people heard silence. I kept trying, but no sound came out of my mouth. Not even a cough.

JULIO

That's how I feel when I talk to my cousins who left. It's like I speak "before," and they speak "after."

RAFAEL

Exactly. Migration isn't just crossing water. It's crossing memories.

OSCAR

But if we stay, what do we become?

JULIO

Caretakers of ghosts?

RAFAEL

Maybe. Or maybe keepers of language. Of rhythm. Of the land that still listens.

OSCAR

What if we could carry the island with us?

RAFAEL

It won't fit in a suitcase, brother.

JULIO

Maybe it fits in our stories.

RAFAEL

Then we'd better tell them often.

OSCAR

I remember my grandma saying, "If you don't water your roots, your flowers mean nothing."

RAFAEL

Your grandma was wise.

JULIO

So if we go... how do we not forget?

RAFAEL

You stop pretending to be someone else. You speak Spanish even when they frown. You eat your "mangu" even when they offer bagels. You call home when it hurts.

OSCAR

And you write your name the same way, even if they misspell it or want to use "Ralph" instead of Rafa.

JULIO

I want to tattoo it—my real name—on my chest. Not the nickname they'll give me.

RAFAEL

Do it. And when they ask what it means, tell them it's a the hottest month of your country in three syllables in Spanish.

OSCAR

Tell them it's heat, music, and memory. The humidity, the heat and the mosquitoes.

RAFAEL

Tell them you come from an island that once whispered your name.

JULIO

You think the land really listens?

RAFAEL

I think it remembers. Even when we don't.

OSCAR

Then maybe, before we go, we should talk to it.

RAFAEL

Say goodbye?

JULIO

Say *thank you*.

(They all sit quietly. A breeze passes through the half-built walls, rattling a tarp above. Dust dances in the light like falling ash.)

OSCAR

You think we'll change?

RAFAEL

Yes. And that's okay. But we don't have to *erase*.

JULIO

Promise me—wherever we land—we remember this.

RAFAEL

The pact grows deeper.

OSCAR

To carry the island within.

JULIO

To let it speak.

RAFAEL

And to listen.

(The silence that follows is full—not empty. Not imagined. As if somewhere beneath the cement, the island heard them, and answered in stillness.)

Act Three – Skylines and Silence

Setting: Back at the job site. Reality and imagination clash. Not everyone is ready to leave.

IX. The Ladder to Nowhere

A sudden injury disrupts plans, casting doubt.

Scene: Early afternoon on another week. The heat is brutal. Cement dust clings to their arms. The usual rhythm of hammering and lifting echoes across the half-built house. Then—CRASH.

OSCAR (shouting)
The hell! JULIO!

RAFAEL
Duck!... Aargh! Son of a monkey! Don't move, don't move!

JULIO (groaning)
I'm... I'm fine. I think. Just the ankle...

RAFAEL
You fell from the top rung, dammit! That's not "fine."

OSCAR

We need to ice that. Do we even have ice?

RAFAEL

We barely have water. Here—take my bandana.

JULIO

(Sitting up slowly, wincing)

I missed a step. It just gave out.

RAFAEL

The ladder gave out. It's cracked at the base. Rotten
wood.

OSCAR

Like everything else around here.

RAFAEL

Don't start. Not now!

JULIO

(Sarcastic)

So much for climbing toward a better future, huh?

OSCAR

Don't joke! That fall could've snapped your spine,
man.

RAFAEL

You're lucky it's just your ankle. Can you wiggle your
toes?

JULIO

Yeah. Hurts, but I can.

OSCAR

No hospital, right?

RAFAEL

Not unless he wants to lose a week's wages and sit
eight hours in plastic chairs.

JULIO

No hospital!... Just let me breathe.

**(They sit in tense silence. The sun glares down like
judgment. The broken ladder lies sideways like a
twisted rib.)**

OSCAR

You know what this is?

RAFAEL

A reminder.

OSCAR

That we're still here. Stuck.

RAFAEL

That we're still *mortal*.

JULIO

(Sighing)

This ankle... it messes up the timing.

OSCAR

What timing?

RAFAEL

The ferry. The plan.

JULIO

We were supposed to meet the guy next week. I can't
even walk straight now.

OSCAR

So we postpone this. A week or two.

RAFAEL

Postpone? Do you think the sea waits? Do you think
the "Capitan" reschedules?

OSCAR

He'll take our money whenever we offer it.

RAFAEL

Or he'll vanish with it, like half these shadows
promising freedom.

JULIO

You think this is a sign?

OSCAR

Don't go all mystical on us now.

RAFAEL

I don't believe in signs. I believe in broken ladders
that kill men who forget all about gravity.

OSCAR

So what, we cancel everything because of one fall?

RAFAEL

We reevaluate. That's what we do.

JULIO

We swore an oath. Spit in our palms, remember?

RAFAEL

That was before the ladder reminded us that we
bleed.

OSCAR

So do people in Mayagüez.

RAFAEL

But there, we'll be nameless. Limping nobodies in a
strange land.

OSCAR

What do you think? We're nobodies here already.

RAFAEL

Here, at least the land knows our names, and our
family cares about us.

JULIO

But it doesn't feed us.

RAFAEL

So we run? On a sprained ankle?

OSCAR

Don't make this about the ankle. Make it about fear.

RAFAEL

I'm not afraid.

OSCAR

Then what?

RAFAEL

I'm tired. Of pretending we're invincible. Of acting like ferry tickets erase poverty.

JULIO

They don't. But they buy distance. They buy *hope*.

RAFAEL

Hope doesn't heal bones.

OSCAR

Neither does staying here.

(Julio tries to stand but winces hard and collapses back down.)

JULIO

Damn it!

RAFAEL

Stop pushing. Let it heal.

OSCAR

We wait for one week. Two max. Then we try again.

RAFAEL

And what if another ladder breaks? What if customs catches us? What if Julio's ankle swells like a mango and we're stuck mid-crossing?

OSCAR

We can't plan for everything. Risk is part of the journey.

RAFAEL

No. Risk is part of delusion.

JULIO

Then what do you suggest? We just keep mixing cement until we're fifty?

RAFAEL

Maybe we do. Maybe we rise in smaller ways.

OSCAR

You sound like someone who already gave up.

RAFAEL

Maybe I did.

(Silence. Even the wind pulls back, as if not wanting to choose sides.)

JULIO

I didn't fall on purpose. But it happened. And now...
I'm scared I'll be the reason we miss our chance.

RAFAEL

You're not the reason. Life is.

OSCAR

No. Delay is not a defeat.

RAFAEL

But doubt creeps in like rain through a cracked roof.
It pools. It rots.

JULIO

What if the ladder was a warning?

RAFAEL

You want a message from God now?

JULIO

No. But maybe... a reminder to move carefully. Not
stop. Just... pause.

OSCAR

Fine. We pause. But we don't forget.

RAFAEL

I never forget. That's the problem.

JULIO

Then help us remember why we wanted to go in the first place.

RAFAEL

Because we're tired of ghosts. Because we want to breathe without debt. Because we want to build something we actually live in.

OSCAR

There you go.

RAFAEL

But if we break ourselves before we cross, what's the point?

OSCAR

Then we heal. We wait. And we *don't* abandon the pact.

RAFAEL

Even if it's a pact with uncertainty?

JULIO

That's the only kind there is.

(Rafael looks at the broken ladder, then at Julio's ankle, then at his own callused hands.)

RAFAEL

Alright. We wait.

OSCAR

One week?

RAFAEL

One week. No ferry talk. No illusions. Just recovery.

JULIO

Deal. But the dream stays alive.

RAFAEL

It always does. Even when we limp toward it.

(They sit together in the dust and heat, three men suspended between fear and flight. The ladder lies broken, but the sky above them remains wide open.)

X. A Bag of Air and a MetroCard

One secretly buys his ticket; another hesitates.

Scene: Midmorning of the next day. The sky is smudged with gray. The site is quieter than usual, like it's holding its breath. Rafael, Oscar, and Julio work in loose silence. Cement mixing sounds more like ritual than labor.

> OSCAR
> (Softly)
> You feel that?

> JULIO
> The wind?

> OSCAR
> No. The shift.

> RAFAEL
> Shift?

> OSCAR
> Something's off today. Like the air's already packed its bags.

> RAFAEL
> Maybe it's just payday. People get twitchy when their pockets are waiting.

> JULIO
> Or maybe it's because the ferry leaves tomorrow.

(Rafael and Oscar both stop. The mixer keeps churning. They stare at Julio.)

> OSCAR
> Wait. What?

JULIO

I wasn't gonna say anything, but... yeah. I bought it.
My spot. Cash. No refund.

RAFAEL

You did what?

JULIO

Yesterday. Met the guy behind the bus depot. A
plastic bag full of "pesos" and a handshake. He said,
"Welcome aboard."

RAFAEL

You went alone?

JULIO

It had to be now. Before the ankle became an excuse
again. Before I lost the nerve.

OSCAR

(Sits on a bucket)
You didn't tell us.

JULIO

Because I knew you'd talk me out of it. Or worse—say
nothing and just *look* at me.

RAFAEL

So what, you leave tomorrow?

JULIO

Yeah. Midnight. Cargo ferry from Boca Chica. No names, just numbers.

OSCAR

Damn, d-a-m-n, DAMN!

RAFAEL

You were supposed to wait.

JULIO

I waited as long as I could.

OSCAR

We had a pact. Didn't we?

JULIO

We also have real lives. You see these blisters? They don't care about brotherhood. They want change.

RAFAEL

So do we. But we don't cut the line.

OSCAR

Why not? The line's crooked anyway.

RAFAEL

Because trust is the only passport we've got.

JULIO

I'm sorry. I am. But I couldn't risk waking up next month in the same dust.

(A long pause. The mixer hums. No one meets each other's eyes.)

OSCAR

You know what I bought this morning?

JULIO

What?

OSCAR

A MetroCard.

RAFAEL

What?

OSCAR

Five dollars. Found it at the flea market. Some guy had a stack of them. Most are dead. Mine's probably empty too. But it felt... real. Like a prophecy in plastic.

JULIO

(Laughs)

You bought a MetroCard in Santo Domingo?

OSCAR

Why not? You got your ferry ticket. I got my swipe to somewhere.

RAFAEL

That's not funny.

OSCAR

It wasn't meant to be.

JULIO

What about you, Rafa? You got anything? Secret
passport? A plane ticket taped under your mattress?

RAFAEL

I've got a bag of air.

OSCAR

A what?

RAFAEL

Literally. A Ziploc bag full of air from the coast.
Sealed it myself last year. Thought I'd open it the day
I left. Breathe in the last gasp of home.

JULIO

That's poetic. And kind of sad.

RAFAEL

That's migration.

OSCAR

So what now? You go, Julio. We stay?

RAFAEL

Or maybe you stay. I go.

OSCAR

Hold on—

RAFAEL

I've been thinking. Maybe I've been the weight.

JULIO

Rafa...

RAFAEL

No. Hear me out. Maybe I'm the guy holding the rope
while everyone else tries to climb.

OSCAR

You're the one who kept us grounded.

RAFAEL

Grounded or stuck?

JULIO

You kept us honest.

RAFAEL

Then why do I feel like the truth keeps me here?

OSCAR

Because the truth is heavy. But that doesn't mean you
should carry it alone.

JULIO

I'm not asking you to forgive me. Just... understand
why I couldn't wait.

RAFAEL

I do. I do understand. I just wish we had crossed
together.

OSCAR

Me too. It would've felt less like exile and more like...
arrival.

RAFAEL

Promise me something, Julio.

JULIO

Anything.

RAFAEL

When you step off that boat... remember your name.
Say it out loud. Say it in Spanish. Say it even if no one
listens.

JULIO

I will. And I'll carry you both with me.

OSCAR

You better. We're not souvenirs, brother.

JULIO

You're roots. And ballast. And my reason to keep
going when my legs shake.

RAFAEL

And when you find that job—whatever it is—don't let
it erase you.

OSCAR

Don't be one of those guys who send money but
forget how to feel.

JULIO

I won't. I'll call. Write. Hell, I'll send voice messages if
that's all I can afford.

RAFAEL

You'll come back?

JULIO

Someday. With stories. And maybe—just maybe—a
round-trip ticket for both of you.

OSCAR

Make it three. I'll bring the MetroCard.

**(They laugh, but it's the kind that echoes through
something deeper—grief disguised as humor.)**

RAFAEL

So this is it?

JULIO

Not goodbye. Just a pause between pages.

RAFAEL

Well, I hope your next chapter has shade... and
running water.

OSCAR

Plus, a decent coffee.

JULIO

And a job where I don't leave my spine behind.

**(They stand. Slowly. Oscar brushes the dust off
Julio's back. Rafael ties a piece of cloth around
Julio's wrist.)**

RAFAEL

To remember us.

OSCAR

Or at least keep sweat out of your eyes.

JULIO

Gracias. For everything.

RAFAEL

Make it count, Julio.

OSCAR

And don't fall off any more ladders.

**(They all nod. No hugs. Just silence. The kind that
holds the weight of love unspoken. Julio limps
away, slower than usual, but eyes forward.)**

(The job site breathes again. A breeze cuts through the still air. And in Rafael's pocket, the bag of air waits. Not yet opened.)

XI. Three Goodbyes

Emotional confrontations: what to take and what to leave behind.

Scene: Late afternoon. The cement has stopped pouring. Shadows stretch long across the unfinished walls. Julio's backpack sits by his feet, slightly worn, half-zipped. Oscar leans on a post, silent. Rafael sharpens a trowel, but it's more to distract himself than prepare for work.

OSCAR
That's all you're taking?

JULIO
If it doesn't fit in this bag, it doesn't come.

RAFAEL
That's not true.

JULIO

No? Why not?

RAFAEL

There are things that'll come with you no matter what. Things that weigh nothing and everything.

OSCAR

Like guilt.

RAFAEL

Like memory.

JULIO

Like the sound of a rooster at 5 a.m., which used to make me want to kill someone.

OSCAR

You'll miss that damn rooster.

JULIO

I already do.

RAFAEL

So... this is real. You're really going.

JULIO

Yeah. Tonight.

OSCAR

Same boat?

JULIO

Same shadows. Same guy with one flip-flop and a
limp.

RAFAEL

Still feels like you're walking into a fog.

JULIO

Better than standing still in the smoke.

OSCAR

What if it's worse over there?

JULIO

Then at least I'll know.

RAFAEL

And if it's better?

JULIO

Then I'll miss you both from a higher place.

**(Silence. A bird flutters overhead, lands on a rusted
rebar spike, then darts away.)**

OSCAR

I packed too.

RAFAEL

You did?

OSCAR

Yeah. Didn't say anything cause I wasn't sure. Still not.

RAFAEL

What's stopping you?

OSCAR

My mother's picture. It feels like if I leave, she'll disappear from the house for good.

JULIO

She'll still be here. But she'd want you to live.

OSCAR

She used to braid my sister's hair at night and whisper, *"We are not dry soil."* We're not dry land, she'd say. We bloom when we're brave.

RAFAEL

Then be brave.

OSCAR

Are you coming?

RAFAEL

No.

JULIO

Rafa—

RAFAEL

I'm staying.

OSCAR

Why?

RAFAEL

Because someone has to remember. Someone has to
stand guard at the root.

JULIO

That's noble. But lonely.

RAFAEL

I've been lonely before. This time, it'll be on purpose.

OSCAR

What are you holding on to?

RAFAEL

A mango tree. My father's voice. A small church with
peeling paint that still sings on Sundays.

JULIO

That's not enough.

RAFAEL

For you, maybe. For me, it's everything.

OSCAR

You'll change your mind one day.

RAFAEL

Maybe. But not today.

(Julio reaches into his backpack, pulls out a folded shirt.)

JULIO

Here. This was my brother's. Too big for me. It's yours now.

RAFAEL

Why?

JULIO

Because someone gave me a reason to believe in myself. That someone should have something to remember me by.

RAFAEL

Thank you.

OSCAR

(Quietly)

Rafa, you sure?

RAFAEL

Yes. I'm the one who stays when others leave. I've always been. That doesn't make me less—it makes me the memory keeper.

JULIO

Just don't become a statue.

RAFAEL

No danger there. Statues don't sweat or curse or cry. I still do all three.

(Oscar takes out his MetroCard, flips it between his fingers.)

OSCAR

This probably has nothing on it. Just a piece of plastic.

RAFAEL

Still means something.

JULIO

It's hope in your pocket.

OSCAR

Maybe I'll go with you, Julio. Maybe not tonight. But soon.

JULIO

You'll know when it's time.

RAFAEL

And if you don't go?

OSCAR

Then I'll carve poems into these walls until the rebar sings.

JULIO

I want one promise.

RAFAEL

Anything. What do you want?

JULIO

Don't forget me.

OSCAR

Never. You will never be forgotten.

RAFAEL

How could we? You're the wind that finally moved.

JULIO

And you two? You're the ground that held me long
enough to grow legs.

(He zips his bag, tighter this time. No hesitation.)

OSCAR

You got your documents?

JULIO

Such as they are.

RAFAEL

You got your name?

JULIO

Always. I carry it with me.

OSCAR

You got faith?

JULIO

Enough for a storm.

RAFAEL

Then go. And take us with you—in your walk, in your breath, in the way you carry your silence.

(They form a triangle, standing now. Julio's bag slung over his shoulder. Oscar with the MetroCard tucked in his shirt. Rafael with the worn shirt in his hand.)

JULIO

You know... I used to think goodbye was an ending.

OSCAR

Now? Do you still think the same?

JULIO

Now I think it's a promise disguised as loss.

RAFAEL

Then here's mine: when you step off that boat, the wind you feel at your back is us.

OSCAR

And every time you miss home, remember—we're still here, still stubborn, still dreaming.

JULIO

Then this is not goodbye.

RAFAEL

No. It's the breath before the next word.

OSCAR

Or the silence between verses.

(Julio turns to leave. He walks slowly, deliberately. At the edge of the site, he stops, looks back. The other two don't wave. They nod. That's enough.)

(The cement mixer is quiet. The job site settles like dust after a storm. Rafael ties the shirt around a beam. Oscar sits back down, fingers on the MetroCard. They don't speak. But somehow, the whole site listens.)

XII. The Weight of the Rebar

Final choices are made. The stage blends Santo Domingo, San Juan, NYC in a surreal closing image.

Scene: Late dusk. The job site glows gold, then blue. Long rebar rods stand crooked like iron trees. Rafael and Oscar are alone now. A cooling wind rolls in. The sounds of traffic, waves, and subway trains weave together in the background, impossibly, all at once.

OSCAR

It's quieter without him.

RAFAEL

Too quiet. Like the walls miss him already.

OSCAR

Or maybe they envy him.

RAFAEL

Why would cement envy a man?

OSCAR

Because it'll never leave.

(They sit on a slab of dried concrete. Oscar fidgets with the same old MetroCard. Rafael sharpens a length of rebar with a stone, absentmindedly.)

RAFAEL

You know what rebar is?

OSCAR

Steel skeleton?

RAFAEL

More like faith disguised as metal. Holds everything together when the surface cracks.

OSCAR

So what are we?

RAFAEL

Some days, I think we're cement. Poured into other people's dreams. Hardening in silence.

OSCAR

And some days?

RAFAEL

We're the cracks.

OSCAR

What if we're the rebar?

RAFAEL

Then we carry the weight. Always.

(A train horn blares in the distance. Or maybe a ferry bell. Or both. The sound is layered now — unreal, dreamlike. Oscar looks around.)

OSCAR

Do you hear that?

RAFAEL

What?

OSCAR

That sound—like the ocean and the A train at the same time.

RAFAEL

Yeah. It's been happening all day. The job site's shifting.

OSCAR

Shifting?

RAFAEL

Blending. Like it's caught between where we are and where we want to be.

OSCAR

You mean... like a ghost?

RAFAEL

No. Like a bridge. A place that connects who we are to who we think we're supposed to be.

(The light changes—suddenly half the stage glows with the amber glow of San Juan. The other side hums in gray-blue tones, like dusk in the Bronx. The site splits across countries, imagination, and time.)

OSCAR

Whoa...

RAFAEL

See?

OSCAR

Is that... is that Julio?

(JULIO appears, center stage, briefly. He's wearing new shoes. His backpack looks fuller. He stands beside a ferry railing and a turnstile at the same time.)

JULIO

(Calling out)

I made it! Can you hear me?

OSCAR

Julio?

RAFAEL

Or maybe just a memory.

JULIO

You're not stuck. You're waiting. There's a difference.

RAFAEL

You sound like poetry now.

JULIO

I sound like you, Rafa.

OSCAR

You okay?

JULIO

I don't know yet. But I'm walking. Every day. Even when it hurts.

RAFAEL

That's enough.

JULIO

It is. Come find me. Or don't. Just don't forget what we dreamed.

(Julio disappears into the crowd sounds — muffled salsa, a subway screech, waves slapping docks.)

OSCAR

That wasn't real.

RAFAEL

Or it was more real than anything else.

OSCAR

You ever think maybe *we* are the dream?

RAFAEL

I think we're the part of the dream that never gets written down.

(Oscar stands and paces near the rebar cage.)

OSCAR

I can't stay here, Rafa. I thought I could, but I can't.

RAFAEL

Then go.

OSCAR

Come with me.

RAFAEL

No.

OSCAR

Why not?

RAFAEL

Because someone has to stay and remember this.

OSCAR

But this place doesn't remember *you*.

RAFAEL

Then I'll become the part of it that listens.

OSCAR

Damn you and your metaphors.

RAFAEL

They're all I've got.

(Oscar removes the MetroCard from his pocket and holds it up like a relic.)

OSCAR

It's blank. No balance. But I swear—every time I hold
it, I hear the doors hissing open.

RAFAEL

Then ride it. Even if it's in your head.

OSCAR

I think I will. I think I'll go next week.

RAFAEL

I'll be here when you write back.

OSCAR

What if I don't?

RAFAEL

Then I'll pretend you did.

**(A gust of wind kicks up dust. The job site
shimmers—the scaffolding becomes fire escapes.
The cement slab stretches into a Brooklyn sidewalk.
Santo Domingo fades into steel and block.)**

OSCAR

It's like the city's already inside me.

RAFAEL

It was always there. You just needed the echo.

OSCAR

And you? You sure you won't follow?

RAFAEL

I'm already moving in my own way. Just not on a
ferry.

OSCAR

Then we're all migrating. Just... differently.

RAFAEL

Exactly.

**(They both look up. A single piece of rebar leans
against the skyline like a compass needle.)**

OSCAR

Have you ever wondered if the rebar's pointing
somewhere?

RAFAEL

Not where, but *why*.

OSCAR

Then what's the why?

RAFAEL

To hold. To carry. To not bend even when poured
over.

OSCAR

That's heavy.

RAFAEL

That's who we are.

(A final light shift. The job site becomes a borderless stage—one part Santo Domingo, one part San Juan, one part NYC. The men stand between all three, holding rebar like a staff, like memory.)

OSCAR

So this is goodbye?

RAFAEL

No. This is the part where we stop needing permission.

OSCAR

From who?

RAFAEL

From fear. From silence. From ghosts.

OSCAR

Then let's build something. Even if it's just a name that lasts.

RAFAEL

Or a story someone remembers.

(They tap their fists together. The final rebar clang echoes like a bell—boat horn, subway bell, church chime—all in one.)

RAFAEL

To Julio.

OSCAR

To what we carry.

BOTH

To the ones who leave. And the ones who stay.

(Lights down. Sound of waves, train brakes, distant bachata. A breeze blows across an imaginary sea.)

The End

Outstanding Immigrants from the Dominican Republic

By Onairam Seyer

Fame, Fortune, and Intellectual Legacy

The Dominican Republic, a Caribbean nation known for its rich culture, music, and history, has produced an impressive diaspora. Among the millions who have immigrated to the United States over the past century, a select few have achieved remarkable success. These individuals have not only overcome barriers often faced by immigrants—such as language, poverty, and marginalization—but have also left a lasting impact on American society through fame, wealth, and intellectual contributions.

This list even excludes children of Dominican parents born in the U.S., like Cardi B, Romeo Santos, or Zoe Saldana. So, let's look at some of the most notable Dominican immigrants in the U.S.—those whose talents have made them famous celebrities and those whose scholarly and scientific achievements have gained recognition in academia, science, and public service in the United States.

Icons of Fame and Fortune

Oscar de la Renta: Fashion's Elegant Revolutionary

Born in Santo Domingo in 1932, Oscar de la Renta moved to the United States after studying design in Spain and working at Parisian fashion houses. By the 1960s, he had become the couturier for American first ladies, celebrities, and royalty. His designs adorned women like Jacqueline Kennedy, Nancy Reagan, and Beyoncé.

De la Renta's influence went beyond fabric and fashion. He was a supporter of the arts and education, backing young designers and contributing to philanthropic causes in both the U.S. and the Dominican Republic. His sophisticated aesthetic and skill at blending European craftsmanship with Caribbean flair made him one of the most respected Dominican immigrants in U.S. history.

David Ortiz: The Baseball Legend

Perhaps the most beloved Dominican immigrant in American sports, David Américo Ortiz Arias, affectionately known as Big Papi, moved from Santo Domingo and became one of Major League Baseball's most iconic sluggers. After starting his professional career in the minor leagues, Ortiz eventually joined the Boston Red Sox, where he became a symbol of triumph, perseverance, and redemption.

Ortiz's story is one of resilience. After early career setbacks, he became a clutch hitter, leading the Red Sox to three World Series titles (2004, 2007, and 2013), ending the franchise's 86-year title drought. His charisma, along with his philanthropic work through the David Ortiz Children's Fund, which supports children needing cardiac care in the U.S. and the Dominican Republic, highlights his broader impact.

In 2022, Ortiz was inducted into the National Baseball Hall of Fame, becoming only the fourth Dominican-born player to earn this honor, solidifying his legacy in both sports and cultural history.

Julia Álvarez: Literary Trailblazer

Born in New York but raised in the Dominican Republic until political turmoil forced her family to flee to the U.S., **Julia Álvarez** became one of the most influential Latina writers in American literature. Her novel *How the García Girls Lost Their Accents* (1991) broke ground as one of the first English-language works to explore the Dominican-American experience.

Álvarez's writing explores themes of exile, identity, assimilation, and gender—providing a rich portrayal of immigrant life. In her later works, such as

In the Time of the Butterflies, she reimagined historical events like the assassination of the Mirabal sisters during Trujillo's dictatorship. Through her poetic prose and courageous storytelling, Álvarez raised the profile of Dominicans in American literature.

Giants of Intelligence and Innovation

Dr. Pedro José Greer: Medicine and Social Justice

Dr. Pedro "Joe" Greer, born to Dominican and Cuban parents, is a physician and educator whose work in medical outreach and health equity earned him a MacArthur "Genius" Grant in 1993. Although Greer was born in the U.S., his Dominican heritage and advocacy for underserved Latinx and immigrant communities in Miami make him a key figure in the Dominican-American intellectual story.

Greer established Camillus Health Concern, a clinic for the homeless, and was later appointed by President Obama to the National Health Care Reform Task Force. Today, as Dean of Roseman University College of Medicine, he continues to promote equity-focused medical education.

Dr. Ramón Tallaj: Medicine, Policy, and Dominican Advocacy

Immigrating to the United States in the 1990s, Dr. Ramón Tallaj started as a private practitioner but quickly became a visionary leader in healthcare. He established Somos Community Care, a network of over 2,500 physicians serving underserved populations, including large Dominican communities in New York.

Tallaj's work highlights the intellectual leadership of Dominican immigrants in the U.S. healthcare system. He has been recognized for bridging language and cultural gaps in healthcare access, especially during the COVID-19 pandemic, when his organization played a crucial role in testing and vaccination outreach in immigrant neighborhoods.

Dr. Ligia Domenech: Mathematical Intelligence and Education

Dr. Ligia Domenech, a Dominican immigrant and Harvard-trained mathematician, is a lesser-known but equally important figure. Specializing in abstract algebra and topology, Domenech has committed her academic career to teaching and advocating for Latinx women in STEM.

Her career in higher education—teaching at major American universities—alongside her mentorship work in organizations like SACNAS (Society for Advancement of Chicanos/Hispanics and Native Americans in Science) exemplifies how Dominican immigrants contribute to the long-term diversification of American intellectual and academic spaces.

Dr. Yomaira Figueroa-Vásquez: Scholar of Diaspora and Decolonial Thought

Although born in the U.S., Dr. Yomaira Figueroa-Vásquez is of Dominican descent and is recognized as one of the most influential Dominican-American scholars in decolonial theory and Afro-Caribbean literature. Her work, including the acclaimed book Decolonizing Diasporas, explores the intersections of race, identity, and belonging in Afro-Latinx diasporic narratives.

Through her teaching, publications, and community-engaged scholarship, Dr. Figueroa-Vásquez has paved a path for Dominican scholars exploring the complex politics of identity and migration, further strengthening the Dominican contribution to U.S. academic thought.

From Margins to Legacy: The Immigrant Journey

The journeys of these Dominican immigrants are stories of resilience, transformation, and transcendence. They arrived in a country where their ethnicity was often misunderstood, their accents mocked, and their communities underserved. Yet through brilliance—be it artistic, athletic, or academic—they uplifted themselves and those around them.

Dominican migration to the United States greatly increased after the 1961 assassination of dictator Rafael Leonidas Trujillo, followed by U.S. intervention in 1965. Political instability and economic hardship prompted thousands to settle in New York City, especially in Washington Heights, as well as in cities such as Miami in Florida, Boston, Lynn, and Lawrence, in Massachusetts.

Over time, Dominicans in the U.S. built strong communities and institutions. Groups like the Dominican American National Roundtable and the CUNY Dominican Studies Institute have played a key role in preserving history and raising awareness. These networks, along with family and transnational connections, have established a supportive foundation for many of the individuals mentioned earlier.

These Dominican Immigrants Have Become Symbols of Possibilities

The stories of David Ortiz (baseball player), Julia Álvarez (writer), and Oscar de la Renta (designer) have illuminated the triumphs of Dominican immigrants who achieved fame and fortune through excellence in their crafts. Meanwhile, intellectuals like Dr. Tallaj and Dr. Greer exemplify how Dominican immigrants have shaped medicine, education, and social justice in the U.S.

Together, these figures create a mosaic of Dominican excellence—icons who broke down systemic barriers, redefined immigrant achievement, and inspired future generations. They represent not only the opportunities available to those who cross borders but also the richness that immigrants contribute to the United States when given the chance to succeed.

Foreword

by Dr. T. Pires Zalla

"Between Cement and Sky – A Literary Analysis of "In Duarte's Homeland"

Summary of Roles in the Dramatic Structure

Character	Function	Role
Rafael	Moral compass, memory keeper	Roots, reflection
Oscar	Bridge character, tension holder	Restlessness, humor, in-between states
Julio	Catalyst for movement and change	Hope, transformation
Secondary Characters	Backstory providers, stakes enforcers	Emotional weight of migration

I've always believed that migration isn't a departure. It's more like a negotiation between memory and movement (or something similar).

Miguel Reyes-Mariano's stage play "In Duarte's Homeland" is a poignant, lyrical, and haunting meditation on migration, masculinity, and collective memory. Set against the backdrop of a construction site in Santo Domingo, the play follows three working-class Dominican men—Rafael, Oscar, and Julio—whose dreams of migrating to Puerto Rico and New York City echo the historical paths of Caribbean labor migrations while reflecting the complex psychological realities that come with such displacements. Far from being a straightforward migration story, "In Duarte's Homeland" constructs an experiential and internal map of longing, hesitation, and rupture through rich dialogues, symbolic landscapes, and surreal juxtapositions.

The Dramaturgy of Displacement

The play's main idea—a "ladder" reaching toward the mythic North—evokes what Homi Bhabha (1994) calls the "third space of enunciation," a place of hybridity where the migrant is stuck between leaving and arriving, between cultural origin and imagined destination. The construction site becomes a symbol for the incomplete, fragile scaffolding of migrant identity: something being built, constantly changing, never fully finished.

From the opening scene, Reyes-Mariano reveals the layered tensions beneath casual banter. The men joke about digging to New York ("If we dig deep enough, we might hit New York from here"), but beneath the humor lies a sense of existential weariness. These workers bear the weight of physical labor and unfulfilled promises. Their workplace, covered in dust and rebar, is not only a real location but also a metaphysical stage where "mental landscapes" clash with imagined border crossings.

The Poetics of Waiting

Time in "In Duarte's Homeland" is nonlinear. The twelve scenes exist within a liminal temporality that keeps characters suspended between "Crossing Without Moving" and "The Weight of the Rebar." Waiting becomes both a state of being and a narrative force. This aligns with the literary trope of "waiting as resistance" described in diasporic literature (Chambers, 1994). Rafael, the eldest of the three, embodies this idea most strongly. His choice to stay is not a failure to act but a conscious act of remembrance and resistance.

"Someone has to stay and remember."

This act of remembrance connects to what José Esteban Muñoz (2009) calls "ephemeral archives," where queer and diasporic subjects preserve memory through gestures, words, and emotions rather than institutional records. Rafael is the "rebar" of the narrative—silent, steady, foundational.

Migration as Identity Performance

Julio, the youngest, embodies the youthful, eager drive to explore new places. His fantasies are vivid and cinematic: ferry engines, docks in Mayagüez, footsteps on subway stairs. These visions reflect what Appadurai (1996) calls the "imagined worlds" of the modern migrant—worlds shaped through media, storytelling, and rumor. Julio's belief in reinvention is both a survival tactic and a part of his personal story. Yet even he knows that arriving might require an act of forgetting.

"Maybe New York is just another name for calamities."

Oscar, the intermediary figure, represents the tension between movement and rootedness. His symbolic MetroCard—a worthless plastic token bought at a flea market—demonstrates the fragile faith migrants place in objects and symbols. Like the famous coin toss in Beckett's *Waiting for Godot*, the

MetroCard reveals no real outcome, only a metaphor for transit delayed.

Migration here is more than just about geography. It is what Stuart Hall (1990) describes as a constant positioning—an identity that is "not fixed in some essentialized past, but subject to the continuous 'play' of history, culture, and power."

Language, Silence, and Diasporic Masculinity

Language in "In Duarte's Homeland" is sparse and rhythmic, shaped by speech and cultural rhythm. Reyes-Mariano creates space for silences that pulse with emotional significance. The men show care not through physical affection but by sharing water, tying bandanas, and using rebar metaphors. These quiet gestures challenge toxic norms of masculinity and reflect what Bell Hooks (2004) advocates as a "love ethic" that can exist even among men taught not to feel.

Masculinity in the play is deeply tied to labor. The play critiques how global economic systems exploit male bodies from the Global South and shows how these men internalize stoicism. Rafael's quiet pain, Oscar's bravado, Julio's determination—they each represent different ways of coping with the emasculating effects of poverty and migration.

Surrealism and Symbolism

As the play progresses, especially in the final three scenes—"Three Goodbyes," "The Weight of the Rebar," and "San Juan Mirage"—the line between reality and imagination becomes blurred. This merging illustrates a theatrical representation of what Gloria Anzaldúa (1987) describes as the *nepantla*, a liminal space "between worlds."

In Scene 12, soundscapes of Santo Domingo, San Juan, and New York blend together. A ferry horn transforms into a subway bell. Rebar points upward like a compass. This surreal arrangement captures what Phelan (1993) calls "the presence of absence"— the ghost of the journey always looming but never quite complete.

Julio's spectral reappearance, balancing between ferry and turnstile, isn't just a farewell; it's a symbol of multidirectional migration. He exists in multiple places at once, just like many migrants do emotionally.

A Caribbean Migration Narrative

While Dominican migration is often depicted through news headlines and census data, Reyes-Mariano's play brings the story back from abstraction.

It explores the emotional reality of migration—its hesitations, betrayals, hopes, and ethical dilemmas. It echoes the poetic tone of Junot Díaz's *The Brief Wondrous Life of Oscar Wao* (2007), the political edge of Edwidge Danticat's "Brother, I'm Dying" (2007), and the theatrical intimacy of Nilo Cruz's "Anna in the Tropics" (2003).

The ferry, the MetroCard, the ladder—all symbolize departure, but more importantly, they mirror internal divisions. The men are not only deciding where to go but also who to become.

A New Diasporic Canon

"In Duarte's Homeland" is more than just a migration story. It explores movement in all its forms—emotional, ethical, geographic. It also reflects on what is left behind: language, roots, dignity, names. Reyes-Mariano offers no simple solution. Some characters leave. Some stay. Some change their minds. And that, ultimately, is the most genuine gesture of the play.

As Paul Gilroy (1993) reminds us in "The Black Atlantic," diaspora is not just about dispersal but about creating new structures—new languages, identities, and solidarities. "In Duarte's Homeland" continues this tradition by showing how rebar and roof tiles can symbolize resistance and renewal.

Dr. Tatiana Pires Zalla is registered with the Brazilian Bar Association (OAB/MS) under at least two identifiers: OAB/MS 17527 and CE 27688—Galvão Villani+15Consulta OAB+15JusBrasil+15. Her license has jurisdiction in Campo Grande, Mato Grosso do Sul, and it is also known to cover legal services locally as well as in São Paulo and Pernambuco— JusBrasilConsulta OAB. According to her profile on Juridico Certo, she operates under the entity Advocacia Permanente as Tatiana Pires Zalla, offering a wide range of legal services.

Glossary of terms

April Revolution of 1965
A pivotal conflict that resulted in U.S. military occupation of the DR; frequently cited in Dominican nationalist memory.
See: Atkin, 1998.

Bodega
A small urban convenience store, culturally significant in Latino enclaves of New York, particularly Washington Heights and the Bronx.
See: Zentella, 1997.

Capitan with a limp
An archetype in Caribbean migration narratives—the ambiguous guide who personifies risk, hope, and betrayal.
See: Martinez, 2003.

"Cargo ferry" and "mechanic" labels
Euphemisms in informal migration channels, reflecting survivalist strategies to bypass border scrutiny.
See: Levitt, 2001.

Coyote
Informal term for a smuggler who facilitates illegal migration, used here with ironic familiarity. While more common in Central America, it appears in Dominican vernacular as well.
See: Donato & Massey, 1999.

Duarte, Juan Pablo
Founding father of the Dominican Republic. His memory in the play bridges national pride with modern disillusionment.
See: Moya Pons, 1995.

El Conde Street (*Calle El Conde*) is one of the most historic and culturally significant streets in Santo Domingo, the capital of the Dominican Republic. Located in the heart of the Ciudad Colonial (Colonial City), a UNESCO World Heritage Site, El Conde was the first commercial pedestrian street in the country and remains a symbol of the nation's urban and colonial heritage.
See: Jimenez, 2015.

Floridita (Name of a restaurant chain in NYC)
A nostalgic symbol of Caribbean diasporic elegance, referencing Havana's famous bar but evoking imagined cosmopolitan life abroad.
See: García, 1996.

Gringo(a) is a colloquial term mainly used in Latin American countries to refer to foreigners, especially those from the United States or English-speaking nations. While its tone can range from neutral to offensive depending on the situation, it generally describes someone seen as culturally or linguistically different, often white and Anglo-Saxon. The origin of the term is debated, but most scholars agree it existed before 19th-century U.S. military actions and was likely used to describe foreigners with unintelligible speech or customs.
See: Stavans, 2003.

Island as speaking entity / dreams as warnings
Reflect Caribbean syncretism and cultural notions of land as ancestral voice, drawn from oral tradition and spiritual hybridity.
See: Glissant, 1997.

Malecon
Seaside promenade in Santo Domingo, iconic in national imagination and symbolic of nostalgia, departure, and liminality.
See: Austerlitz, 1997.

Mangu
A staple Dominican dish of mashed plantains, used in the play as a symbol of home, identity, and continuity

amid change.
See: Candelario, 2007.

Mayagüez / Boca Chica / Boca de Yuma
Common departure and entry points in the
Dominican–Puerto Rican migratory route, often
navigated informally.
See: Duany, 2010.

MetroCard
Symbolizes arrival and adaptation in New York, and
becomes a talisman of imagined migration.
See: Sánchez Korrol, 1994.

Mixing cement as metaphor
Represents both physical labor and the act of invisibly
sustaining a world that others live in—a common
Caribbean diasporic metaphor.
See: Sheller, 2003.

Motoconcho is a motorcycle used as an informal taxi
service, prevalent in the Dominican Republic and
parts of the Caribbean and Latin America. Operated
by a *motoconchista*, it offers inexpensive and fast
transportation for one or more passengers, often
maneuvering through heavy traffic and poor road
conditions more effectively than larger vehicles.
While widely used, motoconchos are often associated
with safety concerns and generally operate outside

formal transportation regulations.
See: Camara & Cruz, 2019.

Nepantla is a Nahuatl term meaning "in-between" or "middle," used in Chicana feminist theory to describe a liminal, transitional space between different cultures, identities, or worldviews, often characterized by ambiguity, tension, and transformation (Anzaldúa, 2002).
See: Anzaldua, 2002.

Pesos vs. Dollars
Peso is the name of the currency in the Dominican Republic, and it is sharply contrasted with the U.S. dollar throughout the play to underscore economic migration motives.
See: Hernández & Rivera-Batiz, 2003.

Quipes
Dominican adaptation of Middle Eastern kibbeh, originating from Lebanese immigration and now fully Dominicanized—symbol of cultural mestizaje.
See: Turits, 2003.

Salsarengue
Portmanteau of salsa and merengue, reflecting hybrid musical forms popular across the Caribbean and among Dominican diasporas.
See: Pacini Hernández, 1995.

San Juan

Capital of Puerto Rico, a frequent destination for Dominican migrants due to historical, linguistic, and legal proximities.

See: Duany, 2010.

References

Alvarez, Julia. *How the García Girls Lost Their Accents*. Algonquin Books, 1991.

Alvarez, Julia. *In the Time of the Butterflies*. Algonquin Books, 1994.

Anzaldua, G. (1987). *Borderlands/La Frontera: The New Mestiza*. Aunt Lute Books.

Anzaldua, G. E. (2002). *Now let us shift... the path of conocimiento... inner work, public acts*. In G. E. Anzaldúa & A. Keating (Eds.), *This bridge we call home: Radical visions for transformation* (pp. 540–578). Routledge.

Appadurai, A. (1996). *Modernity at Large: Cultural Dimensions of Globalization*. University of Minnesota Press.

Atkin, E. Michael. *The Dominican Republic and the United States: From Imperialism to Transnationalism*. University of Georgia Press, 1998.

Austerlitz, Paul. *Merengue: Dominican Music and Dominican Identity*. Temple University Press, 1997.

Bhabha, H. K. (1994). *The Location of Culture*. Routledge.

Camara, M. A., & Cruz, Y. (2019). *Transporte informal y movilidad urbana en la República Dominicana: El caso de los motoconchos*. Instituto de Estudios del Transporte Urbano.

Camillus Health Concern. "About Us." https://www.camillushealth.org

Candelario, Ginetta E. B. *Black Behind the Ears: Dominican Racial Identity from Museums to Beauty Shops*. Duke University Press, 2007.

Chambers, I. (1994). *Migrancy, Culture, Identity*. Routledge.

CUNY Dominican Studies Institute. "History of Dominican Immigration." https://www.ccny.cuny.edu/dsi

Danticat, E. (2007). *Brother, I'm Dying*. Alfred A. Knopf.

De la Renta, Oscar. *Oscar: The Style, Inspiration, and Life of Oscar de la Renta*. Abrams Books, 2014.

Díaz, J. (2007). *The Brief Wondrous Life of Oscar Wao*. Riverhead Books.

Donato, Katharine M., and Douglas S. Massey. "Effect of the Immigration Reform and Control Act on

148

the Wages of Mexican Migrants." *Social Science Quarterly*, vol. 80, no. 1, 1999, pp. 1–17.

Du Bois, W. E. B. (1903). *The souls of Black folk*. A. C. McClurg & Co.

Duany, Jorge. *Blurred Borders: Transnational Migration between the Hispanic Caribbean and the United States*. University of North Carolina Press, 2010.

Figueroa-Vásquez, Yomaira C. *Decolonizing Diasporas: Radical Mappings of Afro-Atlantic Literature*. Northwestern University Press, 2020.

García Márquez, G. (2003). *Living to tell the tale* (E. Grossman, Trans.). Alfred A. Knopf.

García, María Cristina. *Havana USA: Cuban Exiles and Cuban Americans in South Florida, 1959–1994*. University of California Press, 1996.

Gilroy, P. (1993). *The Black Atlantic: Modernity and Double Consciousness*. Harvard University Press.

Glissant, Édouard. *Poetics of Relation*. Translated by Betsy Wing, University of Michigan Press, 1997.

Greer, Pedro J. *Waking Up in America: How One Doctor Brings Hope to Those Who Need It Most*. Health Communications, 1999.

Hall, S. (1990). Cultural identity and diaspora. In J. Rutherford (Ed.), *Identity: Community, Culture, Difference* (pp. 222–237). Lawrence & Wishart.

Hernández, Ramona, and Francisco L. Rivera-Batiz. *Dominicans in the United States: A Socioeconomic Profile, 2000*. Dominican Studies Institute, CUNY, 2003.

Hirsch, M. (1997). *Family frames: Photography, narrative, and postmemory*. Harvard University Press.

Jimenez, M. (2015). *Calle El Conde: entre la memoria y la modernidad*. Archivo General de la Nacion.

Hooks, B. (2004). *The Will to Change: Men, Masculinity, and Love*. Atria Books.

Levitt, Peggy. *The Transnational Villagers*. University of California Press, 2001.

Martinez, Samuel. "Not a Cockfight: Rethinking Haitian–Dominican Relations." *Latin American Perspectives*, vol. 30, no. 3, 2003, pp. 80–101.

MLB Hall of Fame. "David Ortiz Induction." https://baseballhall.org/hall-of-famers/ortiz-david

Moya Pons, Frank. *The Dominican Republic: A National History*. Markus Wiener Publishers, 1995.

Muñoz, J. E. (2009). *Cruising Utopia: The Then and There of Queer Futurity*. NYU Press.

Pacini Hernández, Deborah. *Bachata: A Social History of Dominican Popular Music*. Temple University Press, 1995.

Pew Research Center. "Dominican Immigrants in the U.S." 2021. https://www.pewresearch.org

Phelan, P. (1993). *Unmarked: The Politics of Performance*. Routledge.

Sanchez Korrol, Virginia. *From Colonia to Community: The History of Puerto Ricans in New York City*. University of California Press, 1994.

Sheller, Mimi. *Consuming the Caribbean: From Arawaks to Zombies*. Routledge, 2003.

Somos Community Care. "Who We Are." https://somoscommunitycare.org

Stavans, I. (2003). *Spanglish: The Making of a New American Language*. HarperCollins.

Turits, Richard Lee. *Foundations of Despotism: Peasants, the Trujillo Regime, and Modernity in Dominican History*. Stanford University Press, 2003.

U.S. Census Bureau. *American Community Survey: Dominican Population Estimates*. 2020.

Villalona, Jose. "From the Quisqueya Heights to the Bronx: Dominican American Political

Influence." *Centro Journal*, vol. 29, no. 1, 2017, pp. 56–72.

Zentella, Ana Celia. *Growing Up Bilingual: Puerto Rican Children in New York*. Blackwell, 1997.

rev.08.25.2025

In the blistering heat of Santo Domingo's construction sites, three laborers mix cement and sweat while dreaming of faraway shores. Beneath their laughter lie aching questions about migration, manhood, and memory. Foundations and Farewells capture the beauty and burden of hope, as each shovel of dirt uncovers both possibility and pain intertwine.

Dr. O. Wang

www.ingramcontent.com/pod-product-compliance
Lightning Source LLC
Chambersburg PA
CBHW070333130626
46556CB00007B/2841